SAMURAI STRIKE

By Ace Landers

SCHOLASTIC INC.

New York   Toronto   London   Auckland
Sydney   Mexico City   New Delhi   Hong Kong

ISBN 978-0-545-40322-1

12 11 10 9 8 7 6 5 4 3   12 13 14 15 16 17/0

Printed in the U.S.A.
First printing, August 2012

One day, the Power Ranger Samurai were in the city when Emily noticed something.

"Can it be . . . ?" Emily asked as she leaned over a pool of red water.

"That's Sanzu River water," said Jayden.

"With pools like these, the Nighlok can rehydrate without even going back to the Netherworld," said Kevin.

"The last time this happened, Mentor Ji said that it was a sign that the Nighlok were growing stronger," said Kevin.

"And it gets worse. Look!" cried Mia. She pointed to a trail of red footprints.

Those tracks belonged to Arachnitor. This Nighlok was a traitor and so Master Xandred had banished him from the Netherworld!

The Rangers followed the footprints to find the banished Nighlok. But when the footprints led into the woods, they became hard to find.

"Do you know which way he went?" Jayden asked Mike.

"The forest is my turf. I can still track him," said Mike. "He's this way!"

Mike led the other Rangers right to Arachnitor. He was terrorizing a village of people.

"Hold it right there, Nighlok," barked the Red Ranger.

"Samuraizer!" shouted the Power Ranger Samurai in unison as they begin their transformation. "Go, go Samurai!"

"Let's finish him," shouted the Red Ranger.
The Power Rangers quickly surrounded the
Nighlok and attacked. Their swords swiftly
hacked and slashed at Arachnitor, but the
monster was too fast. The Nighlok blocked
most of their blows and knocked the Rangers
aside easily.

Suddenly, the Nighlok launched high into the air with a Mega Hop and escaped.

"It must be heading to the pools of evil water to rehydrate," said the Blue Ranger.

"The monster is really strong," said the Yellow Ranger.

"Don't you remember? He's mutated," said the Blue Ranger.

Back at the Shiba House, Jayden made a plan. If the Nighlok needed the Sanzu River pools to rehydrate, then the Rangers could trap the beast by covering all of the leaks except one. Then, when Arachnitor went to the remaining pool, the Power Rangers could ambush him.

Mentor Ji had a plan, too. He went to see Antonio, the Gold Ranger.

"We have a big problem," said Mentor Ji. "Programming the Black Box can wait no longer."

Just like Jayden thought, the Power Rangers found Arachnitor drinking from a pool of the Sanzu River water. There were Moogers with him, too!

All the while, Octoroo was watching and hatching a plan.

"*Ooh-ah-ooh*. Red Ranger, this is my chance to finally get rid of you!" he exclaimed. He activated an evil barrier that would block the Rangers' morphing powers.

The Rangers braced themselves to clash with Arachnitor and the Moogers. "Be ready. Arachnitor's been soaking in that bad water," explained Jayden. "This Nighlok is supercharged."

The Rangers tried to morph, but nothing happened. Octoroo's evil barriers had worked!

But the Rangers knew how to fight on their own. They were trained for battle. Kevin and Jayden raced to destroy the barriers while the other Rangers charged toward the Moogers. The Rangers were extremely careful not to touch any of the Sanzu River pools while fighting.

The Moogers were strong, but the Rangers attacked with all their might. Kevin karate kicked monsters left and right, and let out a yell: "Hee-yah!" Mike blocked and chopped down the evil creatures. Emily and Mia fought the gruesome foes ferociously.

Finally, Jayden and Kevin sliced the two evil barriers in half with their Spin Swords. Now the Power Rangers could morph. Look out, Moogers!

But the battle was only beginning. Arachnitor swiped, clawed, and clutched at the Rangers with its powerful tentacles.

First, the Red Ranger was tossed aside, followed by the Green Ranger!

Then Arachnitor fired a lethal blast of Energy Slash Spinners that shocked all of the Rangers.

Suddenly, the Gold Ranger arrived with good news. He had fixed the Black Box!

"Let's see what it can do!" said the Red Ranger.

The Red Ranger immediately put the Super Samurai Disc inside the Black Box and called out, "Super Samurai Combination!"

"You're done for now, Nighlok," laughed the Gold Ranger. "That super white vest isn't just for looks. I combined our powers using the Black Box so that we can morph into Super Samurai!"

Surrounded by Moogers, the new Super Samurai Red Ranger leapt into the air and shouted, "It's go time!" He slashed at the Moogers with his Super Spin Sword.

"Say good-bye, Moogers," declared the Red Ranger.

Arachnitor shot bursts of energy at the Super Samurai Red Ranger. But the Super Samurai Red Ranger blocked the Nighlok's attack. Then the Super Samurai Red Ranger used the Lion Disc to create a Super Blazing Strike with his sword!

The Super Blazing Strike connected and Arachnitor exploded. The Super Samurai Red Ranger was victorious, but he knew that Arachnitor would come back for revenge.

When Arachnitor returned as a MegaMonster, he had Spitfangs and giant Moogers with him!

But the Super Samurai Red Ranger was not scared. He morphed into Super Mega Mode while the other Rangers remained in Mega Mode

"Samurai Megazord! We are united!" shout the Rangers.

The Gold Ranger also joined in the fight by turning into Claw BattleZord East.

The Spitfangs struck first with flaring fireballs!

The Rangers still needed more power if they were going to defeat these villains.

"This is the perfect time to turn the Black Box up another notch!" shouted the Gold Ranger.

The Samurai Megazord and Claw BattleZord East used the Super Samurai Combination to transform into the Claw Armor Megazord!

"Awesome," called out the Mega Gold Ranger. "The Black Box combined all our powers!"

The Claw Armor Megazord launched at the Nighlok with katanas in each hand.

"Double Katana Strike," ordered the Super Mega Red Ranger.

Sparks flew as it hacked and sliced through the giant Moogers.

But MegaMonster Arachnitor was still on the loose with the Spitfangs. They rocked the Mega Rangers with another fireball attack.

"I'm not sure we can take another hit like that," said the Mega Green Ranger.

To even the battle, the Mega Rangers summoned their other Zords.

With the Super Samurai Artillery gathered,
the Claw Armor BattleZord had a Samurai
Cannon Blaster. Red Ranger called out, "Wait
for my signal, we can only do this as a team."

Mega Arachnitor surged forward to strike down the Mega Rangers, but with one blast from the Samurai Cannon Blaster, the monster was destroyed!

"Samurai Rangers, victory is ours!" announced the Mega Red Ranger triumphantly.

Now, with the Black Box, the Rangers had an edge on Master Xandred.